ROSEMARY WELLS

Hazel's Amazing Mother

DIAL BOOKS FOR YOUNG READERS
New York

Published by
Dial Books for Young Readers
A Division of E. P. Dutton
2 Park Avenue
New York, New York 10016

Published simultaneously in Canada by
Fitzhenry & Whiteside Limited, Toronto

Printed in Hong Kong by South China Printing Co.
Design by Atha Tehon
First Edition
COBE
10 9 8 7 6 5 4 3 2 1

Library of Congress Cataloging in Publication Data
Wells, Rosemary. Hazel's amazing mother.
Summary: When Hazel and her beloved doll Eleanor are set upon
by bullies, Hazel's mother comes to the rescue in a surprising way.
1. Children's stories, American.
[1. Mothers — Fiction.] I. Title.
PZ7.W46843Haz 1985 [E] 85-1447
ISBN 0-8037-0209-4 ISBN 0-8037-0210-8 (lib. bdg.)

The art for each picture consists of a black ink
and watercolor painting, which is camera-separated
and reproduced in full color.

For Eleanor Hubbard White

Hazel's mother gave Hazel a nickel and a kiss and said, "Buy something nice for our picnic."

"I will," said Hazel, and she wheeled Eleanor's carriage down the street.

Hazel stopped to help the mailman.

"I see Eleanor has new shoes," said the mailman.

"My mother made them," said Hazel. Eleanor's shoes were sky-blue silk.

"Good morning!" said the policeman. "I see Eleanor has a new dress."

"My mother made it," said Hazel. Eleanor's dress was calico with French lace trim.

"Such a pretty doll," said the baker.
"My mother made her," said Hazel.
The baker gave Hazel a buttercream rose.

Hazel bought two cookies from the baker, one for herself
and one for Eleanor, but since Eleanor couldn't open
her mouth, Hazel ate them both.

With her last three pennies she bought some grapes from
the fruit lady and a piece of toast with jam from the jelly man.

"Can you find your way home, little girl?" asked the
fruit lady.

"Oh, yes," answered Hazel.

But at the next corner Hazel made a wrong turn.

After that she took another wrong turn and another,

until she found herself on a lonely hilltop in a part
of town where she had never been before.

"Don't worry, Eleanor," said Hazel. "We'll find our way back."

Just then a boy's voice rang out, "Hey, Doris! Someone's stealing our ball!"

In a flash Hazel was surrounded.

"What should we do, Doris?" asked the other boy.

"If she's going to play with our ball," said Doris,
"we'll play with her doll."

Eleanor was tossed from hand to hand. Off came her blue silk shoes.

"Stop!" Hazel shouted.

Higher and farther they threw her. Off came her calico dress.
Out came her stuffing.

"No!" pleaded Hazel. But she was powerless to stop them.

When they had finished with her, Eleanor was little more
than a rag.

"Eleanor, my Eleanor," said Hazel.

"Let's ride the carriage down the hill," said Doris.

Hazel rocked poor ruined Eleanor in her arms. She heard
the carriage splash into the pond at the bottom of the hill.
"Oh, Mother," she cried, "Mother, I need you!"

At just that moment, on the other side of town, Hazel's mother was picking the tomatoes for their picnic. Something told her Hazel needed her. A drop of rain fell. Then it began to pour and a great wind sprang up.

It blew the picnic blanket over the garden wall.
Hazel's mother caught hold of it but the wind was so strong

that it swept the blanket, Hazel's mother, the picnic basket, and a dozen tomatoes over the treetops as if they were no heavier than the blowing leaves.

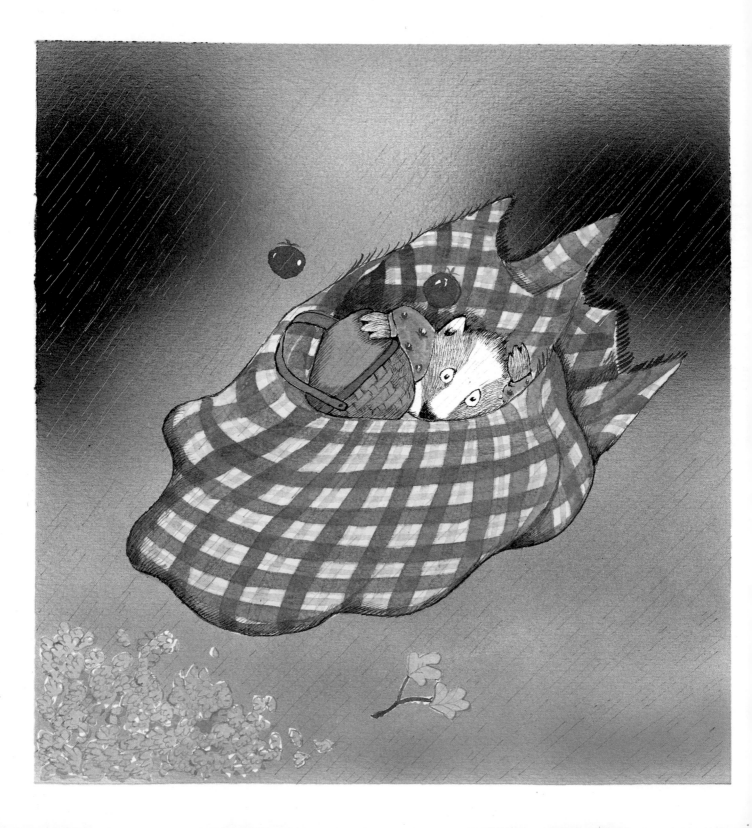

The blanket filled with air, ballooned out, and sailed over the town.

At last it lodged in the very tree where Hazel was sheltered from the rain. Doris and the boys were about to run home when Hazel's mother's voice boomed out from overhead, "Wait just a minute!"

A tomato hit Doris smack between the eyes.

"Don't make a move without fixing Eleanor!" Hazel's mother roared.

"Who are you?" Doris squealed.

"It's my mother!" said Hazel.

"Find Eleanor's dress and shoes!" rumbled Hazel's mother.
"Restuff her and sew her up as good as new!"
Hazel's mother tossed her pocket sewing kit down to Doris.
It was followed by three more tomatoes.

The boys quivered like Jell-O. "It was all Doris's fault," they yelled.

Hazel's mother laughed thunderously. "Fish that carriage out of the pond and clean it up," she told them.

The boys scrubbed feverishly.
Doris sewed like a machine.
Above them the sun came out and the clouds slipped away.

Eleanor's carriage worked without a squeak.

Eleanor was perfect except for her eyes, which Doris could not find in the grass.

The moment Doris and the boys left, Hazel's mother dropped to the ground.

Hazel's mother found the eyes and sewed them back on while Hazel ate a sandwich.

"Oh, Mother," said Hazel, "how did you do it?"
"It must have been the power of love," said Hazel's mother.

Then they packed up and went home.

Hazel took two ladyfingers, one for herself and one for Eleanor, but since Eleanor couldn't open her mouth, Hazel ate them both.

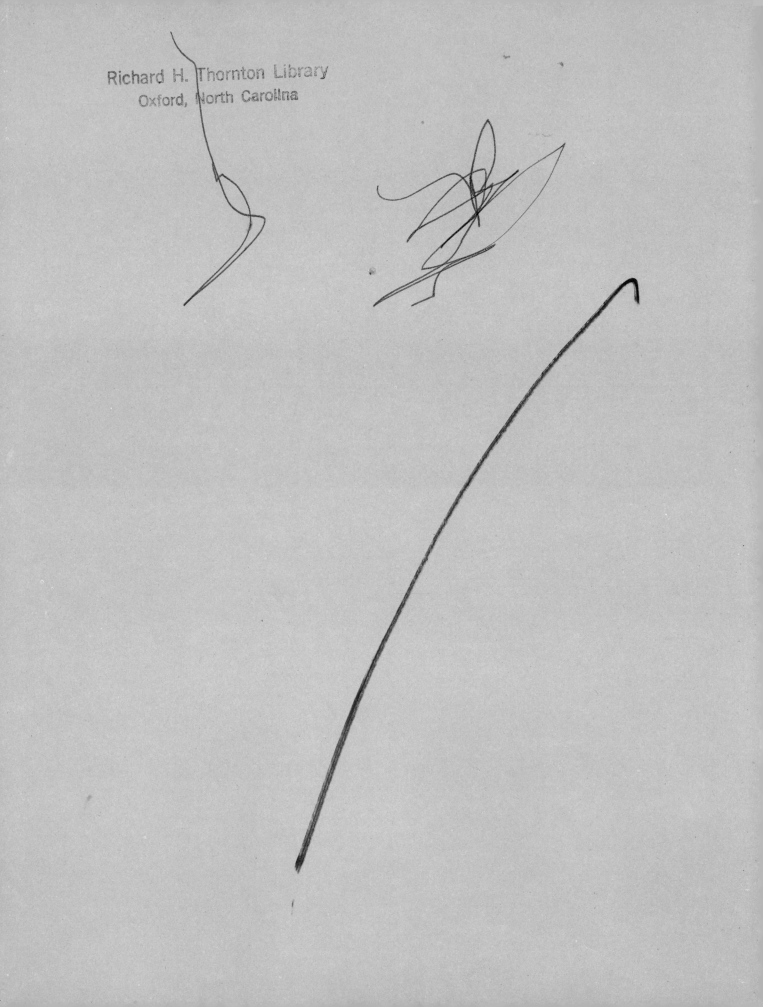